Cynthia Rylant

The Old Woman Who Named Things

ILLUSTRATED BY

Kathryn Brown

VOYAGER BOOKS
HARCOURT, INC.
Orlando   Austin   New York
San Diego   Toronto   London

For information about permission to reproduce selections from this book,
please write Permissions, Houghton Mifflin Harcourt Publishing Company,
215 Park Avenue South, NY, NY 10003.

www.hmhbooks.com

First Voyager Books edition 2000
Voyager Books is a registered trademark of Harcourt, Inc.

The Library of Congress has cataloged the hardcover edition as followes:
Rylant, Cynthia.
The old woman who named things/written by Cynthia Rylant;
illustrated by Kathryn Brown.
p.   cm.
Summary: An old woman who has outlived all her friends is reluctant
to become too attached to the stray dog that visits her each day.
[Old age—Fiction. 2. Dogs—Fiction.] I. Brown, Kathryn,
1955–   ill. II. Title.
PZ7.R98201   1996
[E]—dc20   93-40537
ISBN 0-15-257809-9

ISBN 0-15-202102-7 pb

SCP 30 29 28 27 26 25 24 23 22
4500408499

Printed in China

The illustrations in this book were done in watercolors on Waterford paper.
The display type was set in Cochin and the text type was set in Bembo by
Harcourt Photocomposition Center, San Diego, California.
Color separations by Bright Arts, Ltd., Singapore
Printed and bound by RR Donnelley, China
Production supervision by Ginger Boyer
Designed by Camilla Filancia

For Bonnie
and
For Charlotte
—C. R.

For Aunt Thelma
—K. B.

ONCE there was an old woman who loved to name things.

She named the old car she drove "Betsy."

She named the old chair she sat in "Fred."

She named the old bed she slept on "Roxanne."

And she named her old house "Franklin."

Every morning she would get out of Roxanne, have a cup of cocoa in Fred, lock up Franklin, and drive to the post office in Betsy. She always hoped for a letter from someone, but all she ever got was bills.

The reason the old woman never got any letters was because she had outlived every single one of her friends. This worried her. She didn't like the idea of being a lonely old woman without any friends, without anyone whom she could call by name.

So she began to name things. But she named only those things she knew she could never outlive. Her car, Betsy, had more get-up-and-go than anything around. Her chair, Fred, had never sagged a day in his life. Not one creak or moan had she ever heard out of her old bed, Roxanne.

And her house, Franklin, had been standing straight for over a hundred years and still didn't look a day past twenty.

The old woman never worried about outliving any of them, and her days were happy.

One day when the old woman was out soaping some mud off Betsy, telling her that Franklin wouldn't want to be seen with a car that didn't keep its bumpers a little cleaner, a shy brown puppy came to the old woman's gate. (The old woman had not named the gate because two of its hinges had rusted off and she could tell the gate wasn't long for this world.)

The shy brown puppy wagged its tail. It looked a little hungry. The old woman stood beside Betsy and watched the puppy for a while.

"Hmmm," she said.

Then she walked into Franklin, got a chunk of ham from her refrigerator, and came back outside.

The old woman gave the ham to the hungry puppy and told it to go home. She told it that Betsy always made puppies sick and Fred never allowed puppies to sit on him and Roxanne wasn't wide enough for a puppy and an old woman to fit on, and besides all this, Franklin couldn't tolerate dog hair.

So the puppy went away.

But the next day the puppy was back. The old woman was sitting in Fred reading a book on everlasting flowers when she saw the puppy through her window.

"Go home!" she called to the puppy.

The puppy wagged its tail when it saw her.

"Go home!" she called again.

But the puppy just kept wagging. The old woman noticed that it still looked a little hungry. So she went to her refrigerator.

She gave the puppy a hunk of cheese and two biscuits. Then she told it to go home.

The puppy went away.

That night as the old woman plumped up the pillows on Roxanne, she thought about the puppy. It was a very nice puppy, she thought. It was a very pretty puppy, she thought.

But it couldn't stay. If it stayed, she would have to give it a name. And it could never last as long as Franklin or Fred or Betsy or Roxanne. She might outlive it. And she didn't want to risk that. She didn't want to outlive any more friends.

She would just keep telling it to go home.

Every day the shy brown puppy came to the old woman's gate. Every day she fed it and told it to go home. Always it went away and always it came back the next day.

This went on for many months. The puppy got bigger and bigger until soon it wasn't a puppy anymore. It was a dog. And it was still a dog with no name. In all this time the old woman had gotten a new dresser that she had named Bill, a new wheelbarrow that she had named Francine, and a new concrete pig for her garden that she had named Bud. But the dog she faithfully fed at her gate every day still had no name. Since it had no name, the old woman didn't have to worry about outliving it, and she thought herself pretty clever in this.

Then one day the shy brown dog did not come to the old woman's house. She sat in Fred and watched the gate all day long, but the dog never came. The old woman felt sad.

The next day again the dog did not come. The old woman drove Betsy around town looking for the dog, but she did not find it. The old woman felt even sadder.

The following day when still the dog did not come, the old woman knew she had to do something.

She picked up her telephone and called the dogcatcher.

"Have you caught any shy brown dogs?" the old woman asked the dogcatcher.

"We've got a whole kennel full of shy brown dogs, ma'am," said the dogcatcher. "Was yours wearing a collar with its name on it?"

"No," said the old woman sadly. And she hung up the telephone.

The old woman sat and thought about the shy brown dog who had no collar with a name. Wherever it was, no one would know that it was supposed to come to the old woman's gate every day, that she was supposed to feed it and tell it to go home every day, that things were always supposed to be this way. The shy brown dog had no collar and no name, and no one would ever be able to know these things about it.

The old woman made a decision. She locked up Franklin and drove Betsy to the dogcatcher's kennel. She said to the dogcatcher,

I've come to find my dog."

He asked her what color it was.

"It's brown," she said.

He asked her how old it was.

"About a year old," she said.

Then he asked her what its name was.

The old woman thought a moment. She thought of all the old, dear friends with names whom she had outlived. She saw their smiling faces and remembered their lovely names, and she thought how lucky she had been to have known these friends. She thought what a lucky old woman she was.

"My dog's name is Lucky," she told the dogcatcher.

He led her to a big yard full of white dogs and black dogs and brown dogs. The old woman looked and looked and looked, and finally she saw her own shy brown dog sitting beside a gate. The dog was looking at Betsy parked in the driveway.

The old woman called out, "Here, Lucky!" And at the sound of her voice, the shy brown dog came running.

From that day on, Lucky lived with the old woman, and he always came when his name was called. It turned out that Betsy didn't make *all* dogs sick and Fred was happy to allow a dog to sit on him. Franklin really didn't mind a little dog hair.

And every night Roxanne was sure to make herself plenty wide enough for a shy, brown, lucky dog—and the old woman who named him.